The Amazing Adventures of Sweet Sophia

Sweet Sophia woke up early. The sun was shining, the birds were singing, and Bizzy was by her side. Today was a special day because her class was going to a museum.

Mommy was making pancakes for breakfast. Sophia loved pancakes, especially with a big glob of honey!

"You must be very excited about going to the museum today!" said Sophia's mommy.

"Oh yes!" said Sophia, "I can't wait to see the dinosaurs and the history exhibits!"

"Oh my," said mommy, "that sounds like quite an adventure! We need to get you out to the bus, so you don't miss out!"

At school, Sophia's teacher told them about what they would see at the museum. Sophia's class would start in the ancient Egypt exhibit.

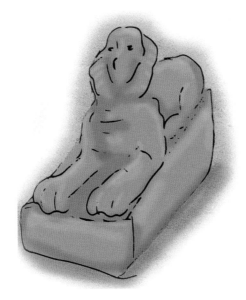

When they got to the museum, Sophia was amazed at all of the exhibits.

There were bones from giant dinosaurs, knights in shining armor, shiny crystals and gems, and sure enough....

there were mummies!

Sophia found a wall covered with small pictures. "Those are called hieroglyphics," her teacher said.

"HI - RO - GLIF - IX?" Sophia sounded out the word. "That is a strange word!"

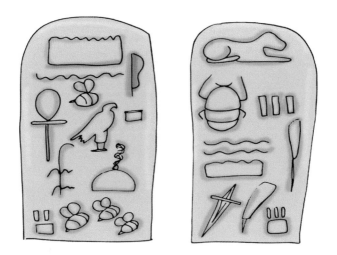

Suddenly, she felt Bizzy start to buzz. "What in the world?" she thought. "We aren't near any bees." But then, she saw a picture of a honeybee carved into the wall.

Bizzy was buzzing so hard that she actually started to fly. Sophia hung on as Bizzy flew around in circles.

Sophia was spinning so fast that everything became a blur. Then she stopped. She wasn't in the museum any more.

She was in ancient Egypt!

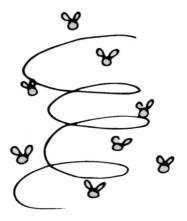

"Hey you! Little girl! Come here!" a man was yelling at Sophia to come along.

He was dressed in the craziest costume Sophia had ever seen. He wore a short skirt, no shirt, and a funny looking hat.

"The Queen needs you in her room!" the man said.

Sophia was so shocked at his crazy clothes that she just followed along.

Sophia was taken to a huge room with a big fountain in the middle. A beautiful lady dressed in a long white dress stood by the fountain.

"Who are you?" the lady asked.

"I'm Sophia. Are you the queen?" Sophia asked.

"Yes, my name is Cleopatra, and I am the Queen of Egypt," the lady said. "I have never seen you before. Where did you come from, Sophia?"

"I was just in a museum looking at these same old pictures. Then Bizzy started to buzz, and now I am here," said Sophia, pointing at the pictures on the wall.

"Those aren't pictures. Those are words. That is how we write here in Egypt," said Cleopatra.

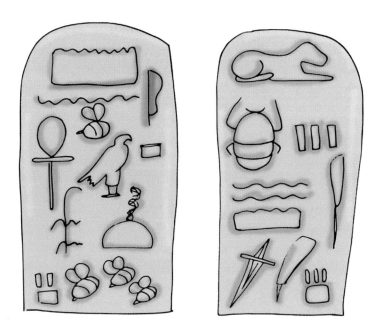

"Do you have bees here?" Sophia asked. "Bizzy takes me to strange places when there are bees around." Sophia looked around the room.

"Yes, we do have bees. We use them for many things. I use honey to keep my skin soft. But we mostly use bees to pollinate our crops," replied Cleopatra.

"Come with me, and I will show you."

Cleopatra led Sophia out of the palace and down to the river. "Egypt is known as the 'bread basket of the Mediterranean,' because our crops feed so many people. But our crops only grow along the Nile River."

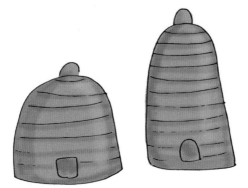

"We put our bees on boats and move them down the river to pollinate our crops," said Cleopatra.

"Wow, I didn't know you could put bees on boats!" said Sophia. "How do they find their way home, if you move the boat?"

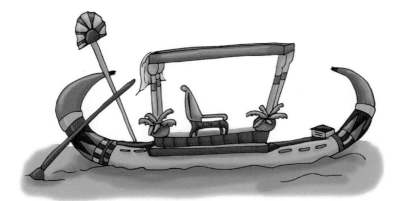

"The Nile is the longest river in the world. It is so long that our crops grow at different times. We just park the boats during the growing season, then move them further down the river," Cleopatra explained. "The bees are smart. They find their way back."

"What are those big things over there?" Sophia was pointing across the river.

"Those are the great pyramids, final resting places for the great kings of Egypt," said Cleopatra.

"You mean like tombs?" asked Sophia. "Are there mummies inside of them?"

"Yes. We wrap the dead in strips of cloth to keep them clean and dry for their journey to the afterlife.

We also put things with them that we think they will need, like milk, bread, and honey! No mummy would like to travel to the afterworld without honey for tea!"

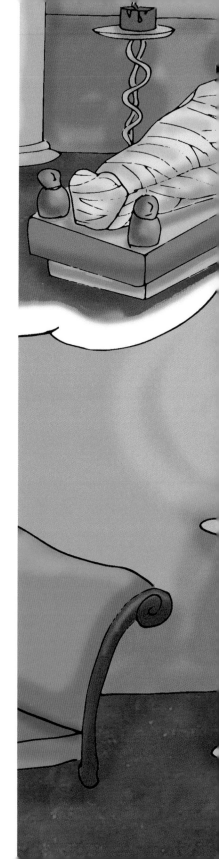

"Let's have a snack, and you can tell me about where you come from," said Cleopatra. "I have some baklava made fresh this morning!"

"What is baklava?" asked Sophia.

"It's a delicious treat, made from really thin bread, nuts, and honey. Try some!"

Sophia and Cleopatra talked about Egypt and America over their snack. Sophia noticed the sun was setting and told Cleopatra she had to get home.

"How will you get home?" asked Cleopatra. Sophia thought about it for a minute, and then she had an idea.

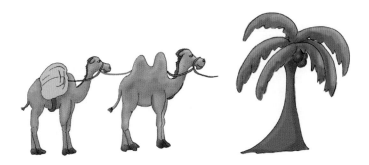

"I bet if I get on one of the bee boats, I could get back!" said Sophia.

"Do you think the boat will take you home?" asked Cleopatra.

"Sort of," said Sophia. She was very excited. "Let me show you!"

Sophia and Cleopatra walked to the bee boat.

Bizzy started to buzz, and so did the bees.

"IT'S WORKING!!!" shouted Sophia over the loud hum of the bees. "THANK YOU FOR THE BAKLAVA!"

Cleopatra watched in amazement at the swirl of bees around her new friend....and then,

Sophia was gone!

Sophia was suddenly back in the museum with her class like nothing had happened.

"Wow, that was awesome!" thought Sophia.

When Sophia got home from school that day, she told her Mommy all about her amazing adventure to ancient Egypt. She even taught her mommy about the sweet treat called baklava!

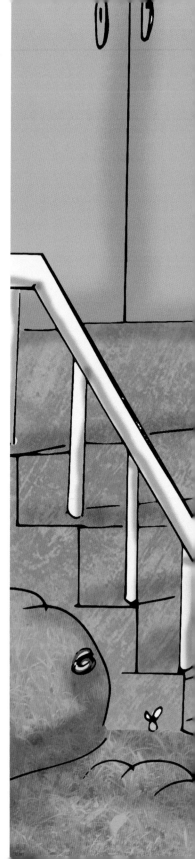

Sweet Sophia's Easy Baklava

Always make sure
you are with an
adult when baking!

1 Package (16 oz) Phyllo Dough
1 lb Chopped Nuts
1 Cup Butter
1 Teaspoon Ground Cinnamon
1 Cup Water
1 Cup White Sugar
1 Teaspoon Vanilla Extract
1/2 Cup Honey

Preheat oven to 350 degrees and butter the bottom of a 9" x 13" pan.

Toss chopped nuts in cinnamon and set aside.

Unroll phyllo dough and cut a whole stack in half to fit into a pan. Place 2 sheets of dough in the pan and spread butter thoroughly over the dough. Repeat until you have 8 layers.

Sprinkle 2-3 Tbs of nut mix on top. Top with 2 sheets of dough, butter, and nuts, layering as you go, until the top layer is 6-8 sheets deep.

Using a knife, cut into diamond or square shapes. Bake for 50 minutes until golden and crisp.

Make the sauce while the baklava is baking. Boil the sugar and water until the sugar is melted. Add vanilla and honey, then simmer for 20 minutes.

Remove the baklava from the oven and immediately spoon the sauce over it.

Let cool and enjoy!

Fun Facts

The Egyptian alphabet contained more than 700 hieroglyphs.

Honey, over 4000 years old, was found in Egyptian tombs, and it was perfectly edible.

Over 130 pyramids have been discovered in Egypt.

Ancient Egyptian Kings and Queens were called Pharaohs (FAY - ROHS).

One of Cleopatra's beauty secrets was to bathe in milk, honey, and almond oil.

Ancient Egyptians thought honeybees were sacred, created from the tears of Ra, the God of the Sun.

The Amazing Adventures of Sweet Sophia

Look out for more
Amazing Adventures of Sweet Sophia
coming soon!

Sophia meets Pocahontas
Sophia meets Joan of Arc
Sophia meets Betsy Ross

and many more!

61400849R00030

Made in the USA
Charleston, SC
20 September 2016